A Beastly kind of Love

To: _____

From: _____

Date: _____

Written and Illustrated by
Cynthia Cebrun

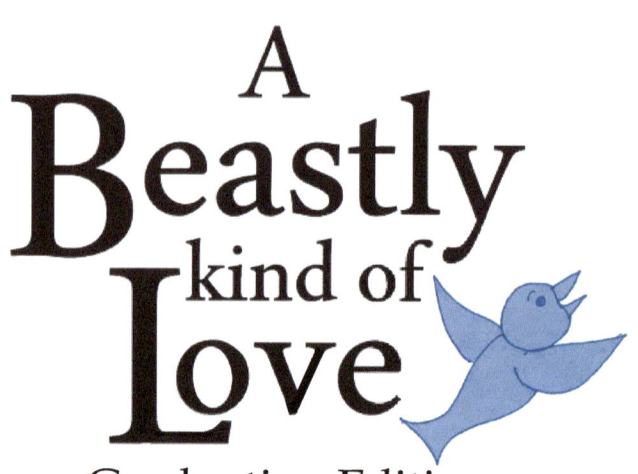

A Beastly kind of Love

Graduation Edition

Printed in the United States of America

First Printing: 2020

ISBN: 978-1-952674-01-3

Publisher: LeRoy Mac Publishing House

Directions for use:

Add pictures and/or words to pages 15, 19, 23 and 27, and to memory pages 31 thru 38 after the story.

- Use glue stick adhesive only. DO Not use liquid glue.
- To ensure pages do not stick together, add stick glue to the back of pictures and place in place. DO NOT place glue on page. (Copies of photos on regular weight paper work best.)
- Use ballpoint pens, crayons, and pencils only. DO NOT use markers or felt pens to ensure writings do not bleed through pages.

---

www.abeastlykindoflove.com

Dedicated to
Lyndia Byrd,
the inspiration
for this book,
and her
grandson, Eli.
And for "Bill",
Ozella,
Wiltessa,
and
Karen & Portia
for your enduring
examples of a
beastly kind of love.

Love grows many layers…

And reaches you in many ways,
My little bird.

Sometimes, love is near,
And there for your senses to hold.
It is the love we see, and hear, and touch.
    It can be a kind word,
    a gentle pat on the back,
    or an encouraging smile.
This love we share when we are together.

Sometimes, love is invisible and silent-
And there for your heart to hold.
It is the love that holds us that we cannot touch.
It is the kindness and care
that was given to you today, or yesterday,
or one hundred years ago.
This is the love we share when we are apart.

This love is like the biggest, greatest beast.
A beast strong enough to carve love
Out of the hours that seem as cold and hard as stone.
This love goes further than any distance,
lasts longer than any ending,
and becomes any type of beast
for any type of day.

This beastly kind of love I share with you,
My little bird, so I can always be with you
Wherever you are in this world.

No matter what happens.
No matter what separates us.

When you cannot see me,
And the days seem like nights,
    with the sun hidden
        behind clouds of stone, and
        caves of fears,
You might feel like giving in,
        giving up,
        and hiding away forever.

But never stop trying.
Remember my love for you.

Love lights your night with memories and your mornings with joy.

Remember our happy times.
They are with you, always.
But you must look for them with your heart,

15

In fearful hours, my love holds you like a gentle beast-
Keeping memories safe and crushing trough fears.
It can bring light and strength in any far away cave.

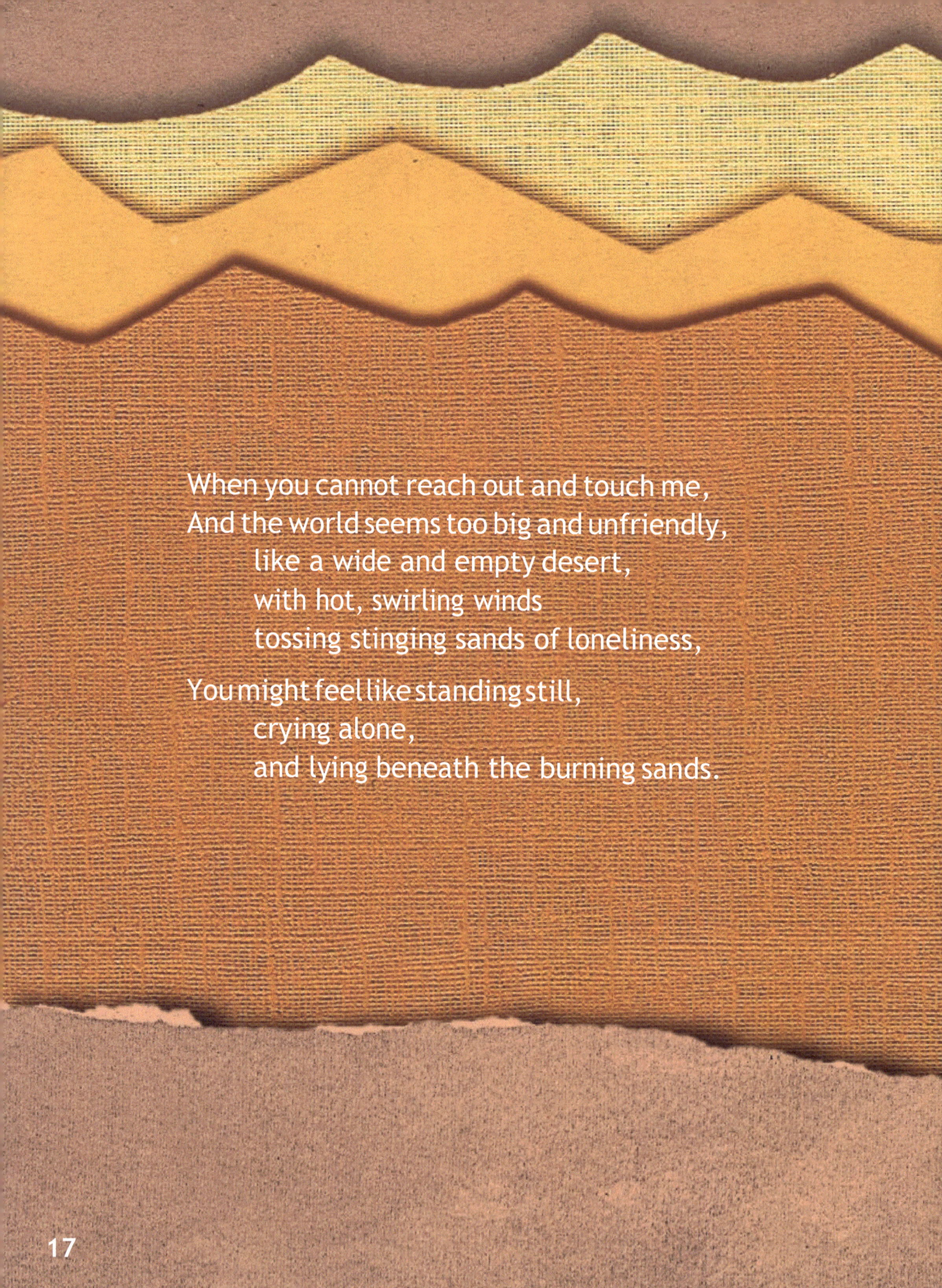

When you cannot reach out and touch me,
And the world seems too big and unfriendly,
    like a wide and empty desert,
    with hot, swirling winds
    tossing stinging sands of loneliness,

You might feel like standing still,
    crying alone,
    and lying beneath the burning sands.

But never stop reaching out.
Remember my love for you.

Love provides a fresh rain of memories to every dry place of your heart.

Feelings from the past are still real, because
Every act of kindness and care stays with you.
Feel for them with your heart.

If you travel over a thousand dunes of loneliness,
My love is there, holding you, my little bird,
Like a tender and friendly beast.

When you cannot hear my voice,
And harsher voices crowd your space,
like waves of bullies rising, and
mean words swarming like sharks,
until your heart floods with anger,
You might feel like bursting forth,
getting even,
and sinking into the rage.

But never stop caring.
Remember my love for you.

Full of peaceful memories · Love takes you to quiet lands ·

Yesterday's laughter is protected for you-
Free from loud storms of anger, bullying, and hate.
Listen for it with your heart.

Love stills rising wakes of a raging sea.

My love will forever sail there like a bold beast-
Carrying you to where tears are washed away,
And a calm breeze reminds you, "I love you, always."

When a dream has fallen out of your hands,
And you think love is lost and far away,
    like a forgotten, twisted garden
    of painful, bitter thorns,
    where no fruit nor flower blooms,
You might feel like fading away,
    falling behind the crowd,
    and being less than you are.

But never stop dreaming.
Remember my love for you.

Love can help heal scars from the thorns of loss and failure.
Be patient with yourself and keep pushing forward.
Better dreams will come, ripe with sweeter ideas.

All the ways I believe in you are planted in your heart
As firm as a beast, feeding hope to all your tomorrows.
For nothing can erase a beastly love once given.

28

Whoever you are becoming.
Wherever you are going.
I will be with you, for I am traveling inside you
in the love that started when the past began.

So, remember, my little bird,
    when the tough moments come,
    that you are held in this never-ending love,
    growing layers upon layers
    as you share with others,
    as I have shared with you,
            a beastly kind of love.

Let **Love** brighten your path, so you can light the way for others.

Show love
along your journey,
and others will
want to follow.

Make sure
love for others
is the biggest part
of your story,
because
every other part
depends on it.

Remember, my little bird,
nothing can erase
a beastly love once given.